Henrietta Hedgehog's

Part of The Homes on Hawthorn Street collection

Laura Kate

MAPLE
PUBLISHERS

Henrietta Hedgehog's Bog

Author: Laura Kate

Copyright © Laura Kate (2023)

The right of Laura Kate to be identified as author of this work has been asserted by the author in accordance with section 77 and 78 of the Copyright, Designs and Patents Act 1988.

First Published in 2023

ISBN: 978-1-915164-88-9 (Paperback)
      978-1-915164-89-6 (Ebook)

Book cover design, Illustrations and Book layout by:

White Magic Studios

www.whitemagicstudios.co.uk

Published by:

Maple Publishers

Fairbourne Drive, Atterbury,
Milton Keynes,
MK10 9RG, UK

www.maplepublishers.com

A CIP catalogue record for this title is available from the British Library.

Henrietta Hedgehog's Bog

Part of The Homes on Hawthorn Street collection of stories by Laura Kate.

www.laurakatebooks.co.uk

"Dedicated to two special, little boys."

Henrietta Hedgehog lived by the big bog
that rotted at the bottom of Hawthorn Street.

She'd lived by it for so long, she couldn't smell the dreadful pong
that made others hastily retreat.

She shuffled down to town one day, fumes, flies following all the way, and popped into the bakers to buy some bread.

Walter Weasel and Marty Macaw were just coming out of the village store; they looked at each other, frowned and shook their heads.

"Really something has to be done, about that terrible, potent hum,
it's sticking to Henrietta just like glue."

They walked along, chatting some more, when tottering out of the doctors door,
came a bleary eyed, sneezing Jeremy Shrew.

"Blimey Jeremy, what's happened to you? Have you caught a terrible flu?
We hope the doctor came up with a cure?"

"Urgh" said Jeremy, "can't take any more, I've never felt so ill before;
that awful stink is worse than rotten manure!"

"We've got to fix that bog real quick, the whiff is starting to make me sick, it needs filled in or blocked up, something please!

Henrietta cannot smell the issue.... Aaaaachoo! Hang on pass me a tissue, I just want to sniff clean fresh air on the breeze!"

Henrietta came walking by as Jeremy made his woeful cry
and was quick to stop all plans right in their tracks.

"No way, you must leave it alone, it's where bugs and creatures have their home,
you'd be taking away their natural habitats!"

Hawthorn Street Surgery

With that she turned and off she strode, leaving scents of mud and stinky toad behind her while the others held their noses.

Now what were they going to do? Something was needed fast they knew, if they ever again wanted to smell fresh grass and roses.

"Frankie Flamingo called a meeting, there was chattering, growling, barking, tweeting while the animals worked out how to make things better.
At last an excited Henry Hare stands up, his paws held in the air and says "We'll fix that bog and cheer up Henrietta!"

"We need to make our own strong smell, to overpower and bid farewell,
to the stink, but leave the wilderness alone.

At my greenhouse there's a solution which will get rid of that pollution
and help to cure poor Jeremy's moans and groans.

They met at the bog the very next day, but Henrietta stood blocking their way,
"I won't let you harm the beasties and the bugs!"

Three fat frogs sat on her shoulder, listening intently as Henry told her,
"Don't worry just get all your old bowls and jugs!"

From round the corner he pulled a cart, so bright and colourful, like a work of art,
"My gift to you is this year's crop of flowers."

Tulips, pansies, sweet peas, daisies, the scent so strong the air was hazy.
"They'll soon bring on their perfume super powers."

"To the bog! Off we go! Everyone pick up a spade or hoe,
we'll have things smelling sweetly by tonight."

They got to work and started planting, soon all were puffing, some were panting
and by night fall they'd worked up a giant appetite.

Henrietta came out beaming and with her came the smell of cleaning,
she'd washed and scrubbed each prickle in the shower.

"I've made some food it's getting late, your work has been super, awesome, great,
I can smell the scent of teamwork in every flower."

And with that they sat in the sun and rested, proud of all the time invested, to turn that ugly bog into a beauty.

Where bees and butterflies come to rest, welcomed as the beasties guests, one and all enjoying smells so fresh and fruity.

Now when Henrietta walks down Hawthorn Street, everyone stops to meet and greet, they no longer hold their noses and turn away.

The bog flowers grow bold, beautiful and bright; a sight that fills you with pure delight, where everyone is welcome to relax, have fun and play.

About the Author

Laura Kate is a Northumbrian farmer's wife and working mother of two boys.

With a passion for storytelling, Laura decided to create some tales for her own children, based on a street of diverse and entertaining individuals (or animals!), all with their own story to tell and a moral to pass on from their experiences. Welcome to The Homes on Hawthorn Street and the neighbours who live there.

Other Stories in the Collection

Handsome Ralf Rabbit

Handsome Ralf Rabbit was quite in the habit of entering the annual beauty show...

Will things work out for Ralf as he plans to use his secret finishing touch to be the best contestant? Find out if he dazzles on the day, or if life and friends give him a fresh new look at the world where looks don't matter.

Jeremy Shrew Breaks the Rules

There once was a street which was always very neat because its residents were super house proud...

Jeremy Shrew from number 2 likes nothing better than sticking to the rules but when his friends throw a party he starts to wonder "maybe it's ok to break the rules for just one day?"

Frankie Flamingo Goes Flying

Have you ever heard of the big pink bird, whose parents never taught him how to fly?

Will Frankie ever feel the wind beneath his wings and soar in the sky? Just maybe with the help of his friends. Join him through the stumbles, trips and slides as he tries to become a super flyer.

Find out more about The Homes on Hawthorn Street at:
laurakatebooks.co.uk

Ingram Content Group UK Ltd.
Milton Keynes UK
UKHW051215250723
425694UK00008B/50